Theo
At the Beach

This book belongs to

_____

who has a great sense of smell, unlike Theo!

Sandy Creek
NEW YORK

Sandy Creek
NEW YORK

An Imprint of Sterling Publishing
387 Park Avenue South
New York, NY 10016

celessence™
Scent technology by Celessence™

Written by Jaclyn Crupi
Illustrations by Aurélia Verdoux

ISBN 978-1-4351-4722-5

Manufactured in Shenzhen, China
Lot #:
2 4 6 8 10 9 7 5 3 1
04/13

Follow your nose, just like Theo...

Today the sun is shining.
Theo wakes up eager to
enjoy the day.

"I would like to go to the **beach**," he thinks.

"I just love
running on the
hot sand..."

Fetching sticks from the water...

and **smelling** the salty sea air."

Theo takes a deep sniff, but he smells nothing.

Theo has lost his sense of smell. He cannot smell anything at all!
He **sniffs**, he **inhales**, he **whiffs**.
His sense of smell is missing!
Where can it be?

Theo feels sure that he will find his sense of smell at the beach.
There are so many delicious smells that can be found there.

He hopes one of them will **wake up** his nose.

Theo trots down the boardwalk. He tries to follow his nose but it's no use—his nose just isn't working.

He follows his stomach instead and it leads him to a cotton candy stand. Theo puts his nose as close to the sticky, sweet treat as he can and breathes in deeply.

He **Wiggles** his nose.

Theo takes quick breaths.

Then he takes deep breaths.

Can you smell the sweet cotton candy scent?

But Theo smells nothing. No odor, no scent, no fragrance; nothing!

Soon his snout, whiskers, and mouth are covered with sticky cotton candy.

"Where is my sense of smell?" Theo wonders. **"Where could it be?"**

Theo *races* over to a beach towel
on the sand to clean his sticky face.

Just as he's about to wipe his face on the
towel, he steps on a bottle of sunscreen

and squirts it all over himself.

Oh dear!

Can you smell the sunscreen's scent?

Theo sniffs and whiffs the sunscreen. He takes **short** breaths.
Then he takes **long** breaths. But he smells nothing.

No odor, no scent, no aroma; nothing at all. "And now I am covered
in cotton candy and sticky sunscreen," he thinks to himself.
"Where is my sense of smell? Where could it be?"

Theo decides that it is time to head home. He runs
down the beach but doesn't get far before he
comes across a patch of long grass.
Soon Theo is completely tangled in it.

The sunscreen and cotton candy are so sticky that the grass clings to his fur.

Theo works hard to get unstuck.

Theo remembers how lovely grass smells. He sniffs and whiffs it. He rolls in it. He breathes in and out quickly, but he smells nothing.

No smell,
no scent;
nothing!

Can you smell the grassy scent?

Theo is sticky and dirty, and all of this
sniffing has made him tired.

"Time to go home for a bath!" he thinks.

At home, Theo jumps straight into a bubble bath.

SPLASH!

The bubbles surround him. He licks them and tries to catch them on his paw.

Theo may not have found his sense of smell today but he's had a lot of fun at the beach. He snuggles up in bed with his rubber ducky and falls into a deep sleep.

Until he follows his nose next time...